Collections for young Scholars™

STEP–BY–STEP PRACTICE STORIES

VOLUME 2

PROGRAM AUTHORS
Marilyn Jager Adams
Carl Bereiter
Jan Hirshberg
Valerie Anderson

CONSULTING AUTHORS
Michael Pressley
Marsha Roit
Iva Carruthers
Bill Pinkney

OPEN COURT PUBLISHING COMPANY

Cover art by Ellen Joy Sasaki

OPEN COURT and ❄ are registered trademarks of
Open Court Publishing Company.

COLLECTIONS FOR YOUNG SCHOLARS is a trademark of
Open Court Publishing Company.

Printed in the United States of America

0-8126-2231-6

Contents

About the Step-by-Step Practice Stories

The Step-by-Step Practice Stories allow your students to apply their knowledge of phonic elements to read simple, engaging texts. Each story supports instruction in new phonic elements and incorporates elements and words that have been learned earlier. The Step-by-Step Practice Stories differ from the Phonics Minibooks in that they incorporate only the phonics elements introduced in the current lesson, while the minibooks reinforce elements learned and practiced in the previous three or four lessons.

The students can fold and staple the pages of each Step-by-Step Practice Story to make books of their own to keep and read. We suggest that you keep extra sets of the stories in your classroom for the children to reread.

For a complete discussion of reading the Step-by-Step Practice Stories with your students, see Learning Framework Card 6.

How to Make a Step-by-Step Practice Story book

1. Tear out the page you need.

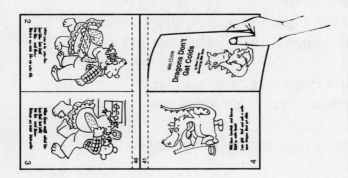

2. Place pages 2 and 3 face up.

3. Fold in half.

Just to let you know . . .

Help your child discover the joy of independent reading with Open Court's *Collections for Young Scholars*™. From time to time your child will bring home his or her very own Step-by-Step Practice Story books to share with you. With your help, these stories can give your child important reading practice and a joyful shared reading experience.

You may want to set aside a few minutes every evening to read these Step-by-Step Practice Stories together. Here are some suggestions you may find helpful:

- Do not expect your child to read each story perfectly, but concentrate on sharing the book together.
- Participate by doing some of the reading.
- Talk about the stories as you read, give lots of encouragement, and watch as your child becomes more fluent throughout the year!

Learning to read takes lots of practice. Sharing Step-by-Step Practice Stories is one way that your child can gain that valuable practice. Encourage your child to keep the Step-by-Step Practice Stories in a special place. This collection will make a library of books that your child can read and reread. Take the time to listen to your child read from his or her library. Just a few moments of shared reading each day can give your child the confidence needed to excel in reading.

Children who read every day come to think of reading as a pleasant, natural part of life. One way to inspire your child to read is to show that reading is an important part of your life by letting him or her see you reading books, magazines, newspapers, or any other materials. Another good way to show that you value reading is to share a Step-by-Step Practice Story with your child each day.

Successful reading experiences allow children to be proud of their new-found reading ability. Support your child with interest and enthusiasm about reading. You won't regret it!

Step-by-Step   A   Practice Story

Slick Sam the Spy

by Terry Fertig

illustrated by

"Where is my newspaper?" said Dad.

"I placed it on the table. But now it is not here. Something is funny. I think I need some help."

"Slick Sam to the rescue," said Sam. "I will help you find the paper, Dad. I am a good spy."

1

"This is an awful puzzle," said Sam with a sorry voice. "I have searched all about without a clue. The paper has disappeared."

"That's all right," said Dad as he rose from his chair. "I can buy a new one."

"Jump for joy!" said Sam with delight. "You have solved the mystery, Dad. Look what's on your chair!"

4

"Maybe you took it to the backyard," said Sam.

"No," said Dad. "I did not go outside."

"Let's check with Mom. Maybe she is reading the paper," said Sam.

No luck! Mom had not seen the paper.

"Don't worry, Dad. I know I will solve this mystery," Sam said firmly. "I am a super spy!"

Sam looked in the kitchen. He looked in the closet and on the front porch. He peeked in the tool shed and under the sink.

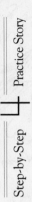

Hardtop's Hard Day

by Marian Harrold

illustrated by Joyce Audy Zarins

Hardtop lumbers through the grass.

He is hunting for tender ferns. Ferns are a perfect dinner for a turtle. Yum! Yum!

Yes! Some tender ferns are just past the rock. This is just what Hardtop wants.

1

The girl spots the bird on the rock.

Then she spots Hardtop.

"You sad little turtle," says the girl.

She turns Hardtop over. "There, isn't that better?"

Hardtop starts his trip around the rock. He still wants the ferns for dinner.

4

Hardtop is puzzled. First, he must get past the large rock. Perhaps he can get over the rock.

Oh, no. Hardtop flips over onto his back. He is startled. He wiggles and jiggles his legs. He is stuck on his back at the edge of the rock.

2

A little bird lands on the large rock.

It starts to chirp and sing.

A girl is filling a jar with nuts. "That chirping bird is not far," she says. "I think it's farther than the hedge in the yard."

3

A Fake Snake Tale

by Chris Meramec

illustrated by Paige Billin-Frye

Jake made a fake snake from paper.
"A snake is just a tail and a face,"
said Jake. "This large snake was fun
to make."

Just then, it started to rain. Jake and
Gail ran away to escape the rain.
"That fake snake can stay in the
lake," said Jake. "I can make a different
snake another day."

Jake had his snake when he went to the lake. He spotted Gail on the trail. Jake waved at Gail and ran to catch up. But Jake's backpack was not shut all the way. The fake snake fell into the lake.

Jake's fake snake bobbed back and forth in the waves. The gentle waves made the snake start to wiggle and shake.

"I like the way your fake snake swims in the waves," said Gail.

The Deer Tracks

by Lisa Zimmerman
illustrated by Allan Eitzen

Pete and Lee were camping with Gramps. They spied some marks in the dirt.

"Look! Deer tracks," said Lee. "Let's see where they go. May we follow them, Gramps?"

"Don't hike too far," said Gramps.

"It's almost time for lunch."

1

"It's time to turn back," said Pete.

"It's getting late. No deer today. Gramps will be sad."

The children hiked back to camp.
But what a surprise they had.

"Look who dropped in for lunch!" said Gramps.

4

Pete and Lee grabbed the horn
to signal Gramps and a full canteen
in case they were thirsty.
"Don't fret, Gramps," said Pete.
"We know the rules."
The children hiked and hiked, but
no deer appeared.

On the trail they came across
a black snake, two chipmunks, three
spiders in a web, a green frog with spots,
a smelly skunk, and a slow snail in its
shell. But they didn't see a single deer.

Earl's Bread

by Tess Baker

illustrated by Kate Flanagan

Have you heard? Earl is opening a bread shop to earn money. He is learning to bake bread. He will serve warm, fresh bread. You can watch Earl work as he bakes the bread at the back of the shop.

1

EARL'S BREAD SHOP

What? You don't like warm bread spread with jam? You don't want tasty bread filled with nuts? Watching Earl bake is making you warm? Don't worry! Earl serves cold water. Earl also serves the coldest, freshest milk in the world. So be happy and healthy! Come to Earl's Bread Shop!

4

His bread will be warmer and fresher than any on earth. His bread will be the warmest and freshest in the world. Best of all, it will keep you healthy! Earl's tasty bread will be the best bread ever!

Some of his breads will be sweet. Some breads will be spicy. Some will be crunchy and filled with nuts. Some breads will be spread with butter, jam, or honey. All of them will be yummy and worth the price.

The Cats and the Monkey

by Carin Calabrese
illustrated by Roz Schanzer

Two sly cats had stolen a piece of cheese from their master's table. It was a nice big piece of cheese. But they could not agree on the fairest way to share it. Each cat was afraid that the other might get the bigger piece. Finally, they asked the judge to help them divide the cheese fairly.

1

And so the monkey kept weighing and nibbling. He nibbled first from one side, and then from the other, over and over again.

Finally, the sides of the scale were perfectly even. The two pieces of cheese were exactly the same size.

"Now this is fair!" said the monkey. "I will take these pieces as my fee for helping."

After gobbling them down, the monkey pounded his gavel and said, "Case dismissed!"

4

The judge was a very wise monkey. He broke the piece of cheese in two. He placed the pieces on a scale and watched carefully. One side of the scale dipped lower than the other side.

"This piece must be bigger," said the monkey. "That's not fair." So the monkey took a bite of the bigger piece of cheese.

But now the opposite side of the scale was lower.

"Aha!" said the monkey. "Now this piece is bigger." And he took a bite of the second piece of cheese.

"Stop! Stop!" the two cats howled. "Just give us back what is left and we will be happy!"

"Fair is fair," replied the monkey. "The pieces must be exactly the same size."

The Bat and Two Weasels

by Carin Calabrese
illustrated by Robert Byrd

One day, an unlucky bat fell into the home of a weasel. The weasel was in the kitchen preparing bird stew for dinner.

"Aha!" said the weasel when he saw the bat. "How lucky I am! This is just what I needed—another bird to add to my delicious bird stew!"

1

"Wait! I am no mouse!" cried the bat. "See me flap my wings! I am a bird."

Of course, the weasel did not want a bird in his delicious mouse stew. So he set the bat free.

And the lucky bat escaped again.

4

The weasel quickly caught the bat with both paws. He was about to put the bat into the kettle.

"Wait! I am no bird!" cried the bat. "Look at my furry body! See my twitching nose! I am a mouse."

Naturally, the weasel did not want a mouse in his bird stew. So the weasel let the bat go and sent him on his way.

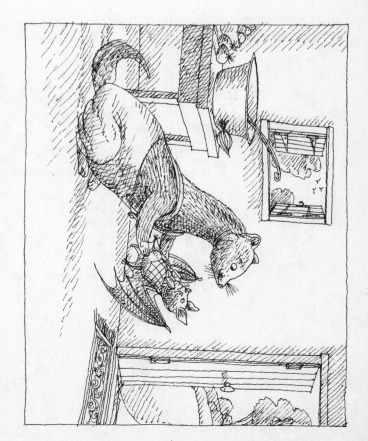

A few days later, the unlucky bat fell into the home of a second weasel. This weasel was not preparing bird stew for dinner. He was cooking mouse stew.

"Aha!" said the weasel. "How lucky I am. This is just what I needed—another mouse for my delicious mouse stew!"

He immediately snatched the bat right up.